Jean Laffite and the Big Ol' Whale

FRANK G. FOX   PICTURES BY SCOTT COOK

Farrar Straus Giroux • New York

He came from up the river—
that's all anyone knew.

They found him on the banks of the Mississippi,
near the city of New Orleans,
just lying there in a basket,
smiling, kicking his feet in the air.

Right away, everyone could see there was something special about him.

The rivermen who worked on the wharves and the docks
took him in and named him Jean Laffite.
They made him a blanket out of burlap sacking,
put him in a banana crate,
and handed him a bottle of fresh goat's milk.

But Jean Laffite would have none of it.
Reaching out with his little hand,
he grabbed a mug of steaming-hot coffee
with chicory in it
and drank it right down.

After three days, Jean got tired of lying around.
He threw off his blanket,
got out of the crate,
and started to crawl.

But that was too slow for Jean.
Standing up
and placing one foot in front of the other,
he started walking, just like that—

and he kept walking right down to the edge of the dock.

And he didn't stop there.

He dived in the river and started swimming just like a catfish.

He swam all the way to the other side and back again—

underwater.

Jean quickly settled in to river life,
fishing, swimming, and making himself useful to the rivermen.

When he was seven years old, he swam all the way up the Mississippi to Minnesota,
and then floated back down,
counting the number of trees along the banks—
which happened to be 58,345,765.

In fact, there was nothing he didn't know about the Mississippi River—
which was a good thing for the people of Louisiana,
because one hot summer day, when Jean was a strapping lad of sixteen,
something happened:
The biggest, deepest, widest river in all of the United States
went completely dry—overnight.

No one knew what to do, either.

Where would they get drinking water
without the river?

What would they eat
without fish from the river?

How could they travel on boats
without water in the river?

And how could anybody take a bath
without water from the river?

Jean Laffite wasn't worried like the rest.

He knew there had to be a reason,

so he started walking up the levee,

and he kept going all day and all night.

Finally, in the early morning, he stopped.

There before him was the biggest, fattest, widest, heaviest creature

to ever enter the state of Louisiana.

He had never seen anything like it before.

But he knew what it was—

A whale.

A big ol' whale.

Even bigger than a blue whale.

It was stuck in between the banks,

like a stopper in a sink.

The Mississippi was so wide and deep

that the ol' whale didn't know it wasn't in the ocean anymore

until it was too late.

A few folks thought they ought
to dig around the whale,
or dig under the whale,
or dig through the whale,
to let the water flow again.
Some folks wanted to blow the whale out of the way—with dynamite.

But Jean didn't see any need to hurt the poor thing.
After all, it wasn't the whale's fault
that the river suddenly decided to get narrow.
Climbing right up and looking deep into its huge eye,
Jean told the whale not to worry.
He ran over the levee and disappeared for a few minutes,
but then he came right back, carrying a small red box in his hand.

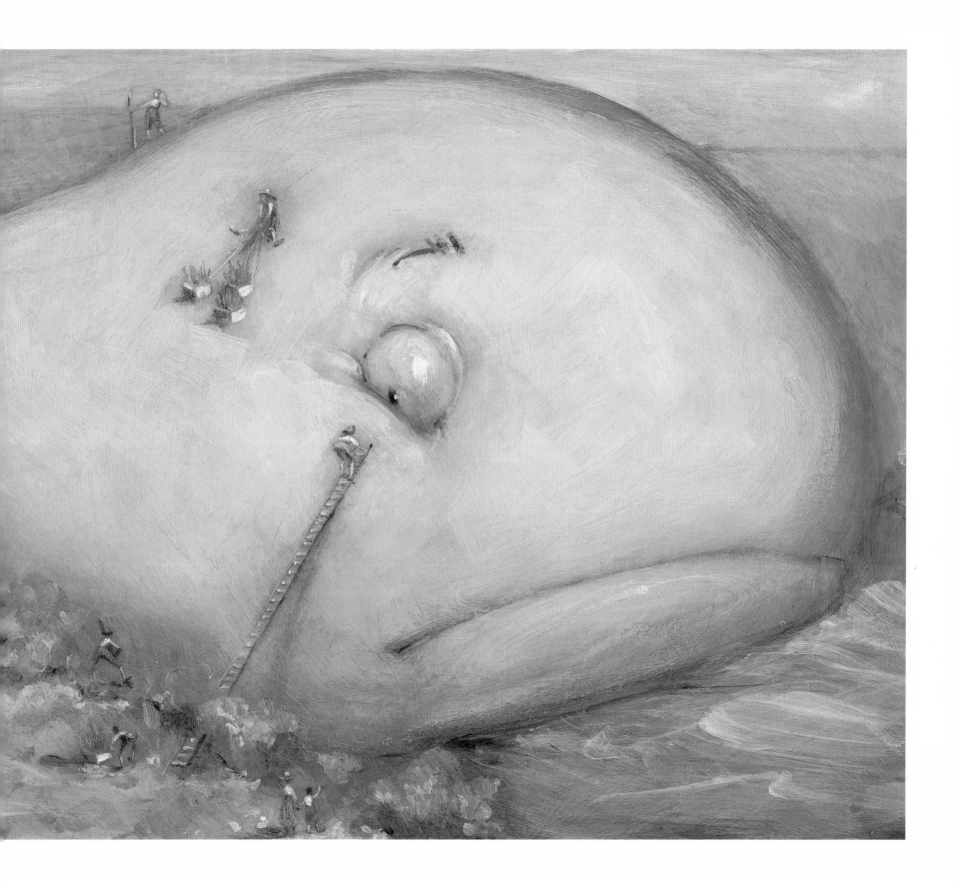

Jean opened the box and took a tiny pinch of something
between his thumb and forefinger
and dropped it right into the whale's blowhole.

That pinch of something was cayenne pepper.

At first, nothing happened.

But soon the great insides of the whale started to rumble,

then shake,

then swell up like a balloon.

Jean hopped off just in time.

Some folks said it sounded like a giant windstorm,

or even a hurricane.

It was really only a sneeze . . .

But what a sneeze!

In an instant, all the water in front of the whale was pushed far back up the river in a big whoosh and disappeared beyond the bend.

Then it got eerily quiet.
But not for long.

Suddenly the water returned,
a great, towering, roaring wave of river.
It was rushing right at Jean and the whale.
Grabbing hold of a flipper, Jean took a deep, deep breath.

When the water hit,
it shook the earth for miles around.
Young Jean and the whale disappeared
under the wall of bubbling, rushing, muddy water.

The people stood around on the banks for a long time,
looking . . .
watching . . .
watching for Jean . . .
and hoping.

But soon they gave up.
Shaking their heads, they walked sadly back toward their homes.
They were glad the river was flowing again,
but it didn't look good for Jean Laffite.

Meanwhile, Jean and the whale were hurtling down the refilling Mississippi.

Jean wasn't sure how long he could hold his breath.

No more than an hour, he figured.

And after forty-five minutes, he was beginning to worry

and thought about seeing what would happen if he let go of the flipper.

But just then he and that big ol' whale slowed down and came to the surface.

Jean looked, and there before them
was the city of New Orleans.
And all along the banks
the people of New Orleans were cheering and hollering and jumping up and down
and shooting guns into the air—
celebrating, just like the Fourth of July.

With Jean on top now,
giving directions and waving at everyone along the way,
the two new friends made their way ahead to the Gulf of Mexico.

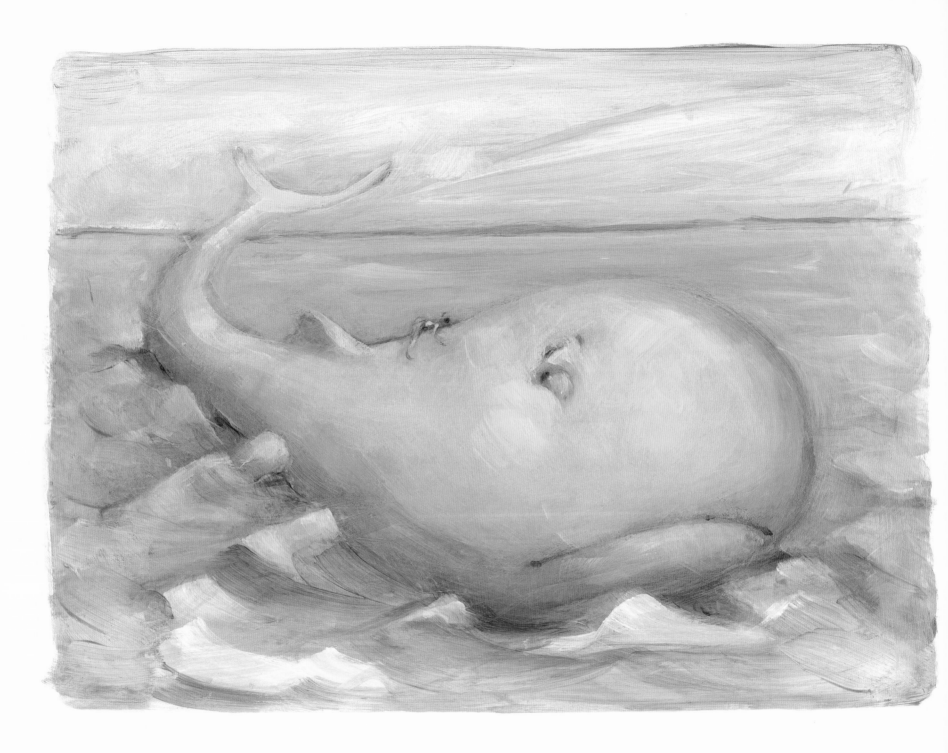

Sadly, Jean told the whale goodbye and started swimming for home . . .

But there was one thing left to do before he could settle back into life as usual.

Jean went out and dug a big hole in the ground,

right above New Orleans,

and filled it with fresh water, plenty of oysters, and plenty of fish—

all from the Mississippi—

so that ol' whale would have a place to stay if he came back to visit.

Jean called it Lake Pontchartrain.

When he got back home,
Jean just picked up where he left off,
fishing, swimming, and enjoying life
on the greatest, mightiest river in the world—
the Mississippi.

Jean Laffite was a real person. No one knows for sure when he was born, or even where. And in the end, no one knows what happened to Jean. It is said that one day he sailed off into the sunset and was never seen again. But we do know two things: he was a pirate, and he was a hero who fought on the side of the young United States against the British in the War of 1812.

Over the years, there have been many tales told of Jean, mostly about buried treasure and haunted plantation homes. *Jean Laffite and the Big Ol' Whale*, however, is a different kind of story. There are no ghosts, there is no gold. It's about friendship, really, and the fact that even the biggest and the strongest need a helping hand sometimes. And it's about a river—the Mississippi—the greatest river in the world.

For my friend Sue Parkes
—S.C.

Text copyright © 2003 by Frank G. Fox. Illustrations copyright © 2003 by Scott Cook
All rights reserved. Distributed in Canada by Douglas & McIntyre Ltd.
Color separations by Bright Arts (HK) Ltd.
Printed and bound in Hong Kong by South China Printing Company Limited
Typography by Nancy Goldenberg
First edition, 2003

Library of Congress Cataloging-in-Publication Data
Fox, F. G. (Frank G.)
Jean Laffite and the big ol' whale / Frank G. Fox ; pictures by Scott Cook.— 1st ed.
p. cm.
Summary: When a huge white whale gets stuck between the banks of the Mississippi River causing the water to stop flowing, Jean Laffite finds a way to get the river moving again.
ISBN 0-374-33669-5
1. Laffite, Jean—Juvenile fiction. [1. Laffite, Jean—Fiction. 2. White whale—Fiction.
3. Whales—Fiction. 4. Mississippi River—Fiction.] I. Cook, Scott, ill. II. Title.

PZ7.F83085 Je 2003
[Fic]—dc21

99-43733